FLEUR

A Parisienne

Haunting

by

Susi Moore

Fleur © 2016 Susi Moore.

Fleur © 2016 Susi Moore. All Rights Reserved.
ISBN 978-1542441025

No part of this work or publication may be reproduced in any form without
the prior written permission
of the copyright holder.

Susi Moore asserts her moral right to be
identified as the author of this work.

PROLOGUE

Fleur Babineaux

Paris 2009

Shopping on the Rue Tronchet was compulsory at Christmas. Here I could hover over the counters of each elegant boutique or salon and find everything I needed to surprise and delight my mother and younger sisters. I spent hours, hand picking perfumes, scarves, soaps and much more.

My eye caught the brightly lit café near the Madeleine. The temptation was too much. I ordered a vin chaud, took a table outside and immersed myself in the spectacle of glinting lights and passersby, all caught up in the throes of their last minute shopping.

I couldn't help smiling as I watched a woman and her daughters struggling with their bags and chastising one another.

I thought of my own mother and sisters. I could still hear their squeals of delight on the day of the final fittings at the Lafayette. Mme Véronique and her assistants fussed and tugged at waistbands, sleeves and hems to make sure absolutely nothing was amiss. Happy with the bridesmaids, it was my turn. I was whisked away to a private fitting room, and, in front of a floor to ceiling mirror, surveyed my reflection. In my gown of ivory lace and gossamer, I should only feel beautiful but instead my nerves churned. Was the waistband right? Were the sleeves too long? Should I have chosen the silk brocade? I could look no more. Mme Véronique sensed my mood and smiled. She set about applying herself with calm efficiency to my gown and then my hair. Finally, I stepped out, in my veil, for the first time, a bride to be. My mother was rapturous. The assistants cooed.

'Fleur, Fleur, you look like a fairy princess!' cried Lottie, my youngest sister, six and a half years old.

'You look lovely too, Lottie Locket!' I said, sweeping her up in my arms. She shrieked with laughter as we spun round and round.

An icy chill brought me out of my reveries. I sipped my cinnamon-infused vin. There was still time. I could go to see the exquisitely lit fountains which fronted the Tuileries. I looked around. Delicate spots of white appeared, rising and falling with the tide of traffic. I became mesmerised. Slowly, the spots grew into specks and the specks grew into a myriad of swirling flakes.

Had I drifted off? It was strangely quiet. No people. No traffic. Only the distant rhythmical clack of steel on steel.

I gathered my bags. I'd barely taken a step when the air became hazy with sudden, searing gusts of heat. I was almost blinded by the onslaught of ash and white hot, coiling smuts. The temperature was unbearable. My eyes stung. My throat was on fire.

Then it came. An agonised screech of steel blasting through mortar. A deafening cacophony and the pavement beneath my feet cracked and splintered. Sparks ricocheted in all directions. Clouds of metallic debris rose and fell. I reached out, wildly, but there was nothing to hold onto.

'Jaimie ... JAIMIE!'

A ringing in my ears. A deafening silence.

My vision flickered between toxic black and the flares of incandescent, blinding light.

CHAPTER 1

Fleur Blaise

Paris 2009

'Nightmares, récurrents … are quite commonplace,' said the therapist. 'Explain to me, as simply as you can … so I can see what you see.'

'My dreams …' I began, 'I see everything … *feel* everything.'

The therapist nodded, sympathetically. 'It is often the case.'

'I experience things that ... I *know* happened before.'

I could feel my heartbeat rising.

'Let's take a few minutes,' the therapist said. 'Close your eyes. Breathe, slowly, calmly ...'

The afternoon sun filtered through the shutters, immersing the room in a mesh of drifting particles. I took a long breath and sank back into the plushly upholstered armchair.

'In your own time ... count backwards, slowly, from ten ...'

I tried to imagine a canvas. Smooth. Bare. Gradually, my breathing steadied until I found that strange, languid place between waking and sleeping.

'Allow your mind to drift back,' the therapist continued. 'Think about the first time you experienced anything ... unusual.'

CHAPTER 2

Fleur Blaise

Paris 1992

My family moved, from a quietly picturesque port on the Normandy coastline to a leafy arrondissement in the heart of Paris. My father was in banking and his positioning near the centre of commerce, or more precisely, the prospect of a nomination at the Générale, was vital for his career. I was wide-eyed, six years old and beside myself with excitement. On the first day, I skipped over the parquet floors of our new home, exploring each room in turn. On the first night, I gazed through the ornate ironwork balcony of my bedroom window to take in the beautiful tree-lined avenues. It was spring and the fresh green petioles swayed gently in the balmy, evening breeze. The cry of seagulls and salt-tanged air of my birthplace was already a fading memory.

My mother crept in. 'You're not asleep, yet, petit Fleur?'

I duly scampered onto my new 'grown-up' bed and sank back into the pillows.

'Goodnight, maman,' I whispered, as she put her arms around me.

'Goodnight, cheri, you've had a big day. We'll do some exploring tomorrow. So many things to see.' She kissed me on both cheeks and left.

I pulled up my blankets, curiously shivering. Was it excitement or a sudden chill in these magnificent old rooms with their tall, tall ceilings?

'Goodnight, petit cheri,' came the whisper.

'Goodnight,' I whispered back, eyes closed tight shut.

CHAPTER 3

Paris 2009 and Normandy 1884

They were fairly short, inconsequential dreams at first. I was ten years old and at the railway station with my parents and younger sisters. Except, in truth, I have no younger sisters. My parents were unable to have children after me. I was too young then, of course, to understand that my mother had had problems after my birth and was unable to carry a child to term again. In a strange way I quite looked forward to my dreams. In my dreams, I had the family I didn't have in life.

They always started in the same way.

'Maman, mère, I want the seat by the window!' demanded my middle sister, six-year old Aimee.

We were on the platform at Gare Montparnasse awaiting the express train back to the coast. Our aunt and cousins lived near the harbour and we made this trip every summer to stay with them.

'I'm having the seat by the window, Aimee. Maman and Papa already said so,' I pronounced. Aimee could barely hide her pique but it was time to board. Mindful of the gap between the steps and platform, we clambered upwards onto the train and ran excitedly through the corridor ahead of our parents to find our compartment. It was fitted with deep-pile, richly patterned upholstery and rouge velvet drapes, elegantly drawn at each side of the prized window.

I quickly made myself comfortable and Maman seated herself to face me. I shot back a look of triumph towards Aimee.

Elise, my youngest sister, aged only four, clutched her doll and scuttled up to nestle by my side. There, I couldn't move now. Nevertheless, Maman flashed a reproachful look in my direction.

'Maman, Fleur always sits by the window,' cried Aimee.

'That's because I'm going to be important one day, like Papa. I'm going to be a director at the Société Générale!'

'And I'm going to have my own palace and guards,' Aimee shot back.

Maman rolled her eyes. 'Let's not quarrel, petites. The train has not yet left the station.'

Papa, who was heaving luggage onto the overhead racks shot a warning glance at us both. 'Girls, don't upset your mother, you know her … délicat condition.'

Aimee scowled at me but folded her arms in a grudging gesture of capitulation. 'I want a petit frère, there are enough petites filles in this family!'

She took the seat at the side of our parents.

I stood up quickly to unbutton my coat and remove my bonnet and seated myself right back down. Aimee would get no chance from me to steal my precious spec. I gazed out onto the station platform to see all the different faces in the bustling crowds, many there just to wave bon voyage to their loved ones. Elise and I waved back to complete strangers just for the fun of it.

Clouds of steam exhaled from the sides of the great express engine and the horn sounded, sending piercing echoes throughout the covered concourse. Elise clung to me in excitement as the train began to shudder. Smoke bellowed as the pistons laboured to propel the wheels forward. Our ears filled with deafening scrapes of steel as we slowly pulled away from the platform. The view from the fought-over window became obliterated by churning, black smoke.

'There seems nothing unusual …' observed the therapist, 'Except, bonnets and steam trains?'

Startled, I opened my eyes. 'I had the same dream over and over, throughout my childhood. It always seemed completely … real.'

'Let's continue … as far as you can.'

I closed my eyes and tried to find that place once more, between sleeping and waking.

CHAPTER 4

Fleur Babineaux

Normandy 1889

I was now aged fifteen. We boarded the train as we did every summer for our trip to the coast. Everything happened as it had before. Aimee and I still quarrelled over who was sitting where, Elise took her place by me, and Lottie, our newest sister, sat with Maman. Our journey continued until at long last we pulled in at Granville. We were famished and couldn't wait to receive Aunt Emma's wonderful welcome in the form of a lavish buffet on the veranda of her villa overlooking the harbour.

She was waiting on the platform with kisses and hugs for each of us. We exchanged pleasantries and how we'd all grown. We could then turn our attentions to our cousins, Helene, Callie and Rupert.

I had always been closest to Helene as she was the same age as me and we had much in common. I was bursting for news and couldn't wait to take her to one side.

'Will … Jaimie be joining us later?' I asked.

Maman swung round.

'What are you two girls giggling about already?'

'Nothing, Maman. We're just delighted to see each other!'

Maman raised her eyebrow and looked like she was about to speak again, but, thankfully, Aunt Emma took her attentions away from us.

Jaimie Luc Bonner was the seventeen year-old boy who lived next door to my aunt. His father was an avocat d'affaires, a career Jamie wished to follow. I'd had a crush on him since I could remember and it was my secret wish for my parents to one day approve a match between us.

Helene and I walked arm in arm, a little way off again. 'He and his family are still away.' She spoke in conspiratorial tones. 'Across the channel, visiting his grandparents.'

I tried not to appear disappointed but Helene nudged me and we both smiled at my dismal failure.

We passed the sunny days that followed pleasantly enough, with walks, picnics and boat trips to the Iles Chausey. After what seemed the longest nine days in my life, the Bonner family returned. I could barely contain my excitement and made sure the prettiest of my dresses was ready to wear for the inevitable get together.

'How would you know this?' the therapist cut in. 'About the Bonner family and the *inevitable get-together* if the dreams had never progressed this far before?'

'It all seemed perfectly natural, as though I'd always had these memories. I even fell into the speech of the day, without a second thought…'

'I see ... curious. Shall we move on?'

I sighed. I hadn't come here to be mocked but decided to take the higher road.

We planned a short trip with the Bonners to see the island ruins of a Benedictine abbey. I chose a sky blue day dress with a ruched, sheer overlay, and we joined my aunt, cousins and the Bonner family at the railway station. I could feel the spring in my step at finally being in the same proximity as Jaimie. I was all smiles and affectations to everyone. I even had patience for Aimee and promised her the window seat. Jaimie was standing with Adrien and Sacha, his younger brothers. His ash-blond hair had grown a little longer over the summer and he flicked back escaping strands from his forehead with a beguiling smile. He saw me with Helene and walked straight towards us.

'Fleur Babineaux, you are quite changed this year.'

I was captivated.

'It's good to see you, Jaimie Luc! We missed you.'

He smiled broadly. 'Well, sweet Fleur, you and I will have to make plenty of time to catch up.'

I was rooted to the spot.

'Oh … yes, yes, well … absolutely …'

I was furious with myself. Why was I so flustered?

I caught Helene's alarmed expression. She beamed us both the most charming of smiles and to my relief, took hold of Jaimie's arm and distracted him with chatter while we boarded the train. I decided to sit quietly, in the hopes of gaining some sense of composure, and nod politely here and there if the conversation required it. Helene kept Jamie occupied, regaling him with different stories from the past week and he nodded and smiled in amusement but every now and then, his glance fell on me.

We alighted the train near the causeway which connected the coastline to the little island. Small boats waited to take passengers with their picnic hampers across to the manicured gardens at the base of the ruined Abbey.

'This spot looks just perfect,' said Aunt Emma, after we had arrived and taken a cursory exploration of the gardens. The blankets were laid and we set about our luncheon of cooked meats, cheese, pastries and crème fraîche. The younger children played chasing games and were chided at regular intervals. The shadow from the church tower loomed as the sun altered position. In a moment of off the spur madness, Helene, Adrien, Jaimie and I decided to race each other to the top of the old spire.

'I want to go, too,' wailed Aimee.

'No,' I snapped back.

'Take your sister,' chided Papa, 'Look out for her on those steps. Don't forget to wave to us when you get to the top.'

Sacha also decided he wanted to join us.

We pointedly walked ahead of him and Aimee as a show of our superiority, perhaps hoping they would drop back or disappear altogether. We reached the bottom of the tower stairwell and gazed upwards in awe at the infinitely winding steps. Helene tapped my shoulder. 'First monsieur to the top gets to kiss the first mademoiselle to the top!' The boys grinned as we all rushed upwards. Helene and I shrieked as we jostled to pass each other while Jamie and Adrien easily raced ahead of us, two steps at a time.

We heard Aimee's echoing protests from below, 'Hey, what about me? And I'm not kissing any boys!'

'You needn't expect us to wait for you.' I called back down. More echoes. 'Follow us. But, *slowly*. Don't run.'

'Fleur, how could you leave your little sister behind?' Helene admonished with a grin but we were too caught up in the moment. We rushed upwards, in our long dresses, as fast as we could, until Helene suddenly slipped on one of the stone steps. I was at her side.

'Are you alright?'

'Yes ... I think so ... ' she said, wincing slightly before crying out. Yet more echoes.

Adrien, still ahead of us, came tearing back down and immediately sat on the step next to Helene.

'It's fine,' he said to me, 'Go on, I'll stay with her.'

Although reluctant to leave, I headed back up the steps, picking up speed and caught sight of Jaimie as he rounded the last curve of the stairwell.

I found a final burst of energy and caught up to him. 'Salut!' We both laughed. Almost out of breath, we could barely speak which made us laugh even more. We leaned over the top of the tower and took in the magnificent views below. We spotted our families and waved to them as they cheered and waved back.

The afternoon light transformed as hues of metallic gold and damson pink trailed through the sky.

We looked on for a while, admiring the pre-dusk display until Jaimie turned towards me, tentatively. 'Well, sweet Fleur, shall we make good on our bargain?'

'Oh … I thought we were just … enjoying the view …' I could feel my cheeks burning.

He laughed and gently clasped his hands round my waist.

I silently caught my breath.

'Fleur, I've always been sweet on you, since the first summer we spent together, when you were only nine and I was only ten …'

'You have? Oh …' It seemed I couldn't stop myself from saying 'Oh' today. Yet I had climbed those steps as fast as I could to have this very moment. Now it was here, my heart was beating so fast I felt it might burst open.

'May I?' he asked, suddenly serious. He raised one hand to my face to brush aside a stray wisp of hair. He smiled as his clear blue eyes searched out mine. He leaned forwards and brushed his lips against mine so sweetly I thought I might die. I felt a sudden rush of joy and raised my mouth to his and we kissed again.

'Merci!' Helene was at the top of the stairwell. Our moment was over. 'Yes, I'm quite alright, don't fret yourself about my little fall ...'

'Helene, your foot? You shouldn't have come all this way up! Are you alright?'

'Oui, oui, sweet cousin Fleur, Thanks to my knight in shining armour.'

Adrien stepped out alongside Helene. 'I was just doing what anyone would do,' he said gruffly, aware of his older brother's bemusement.

'And guess whom?' Helene continued.

Aimee and Sacha stepped out from behind them, breathless but proud at having reached the top.

Jaimie was at once the gracious host. 'Well, here we all are, let's take in the views and then escort these lovely young ladies back down. I imagine our families are eager to get back to our lodgings before dark.'

Helene shot me sideways looks all the way down the stairwell until we reached the bottom.

'Tell all,' she said, as soon as she thought we were out of earshot.

'Nothing to tell …'

'Non?' she asked with a quizzical eyebrow.

'Except my very first kiss,' I said, secretly delighted at being able to say just that.

'Jaimie kissed Fleur!! Jaimie kissed Fleur!!' Aimee danced around us. Like my mother, she did not miss much.

'Shhhhh! You will *not* tell Maman!'

'Or what?'

'Or ... I will ... You little beast. How about I let you sit by the window on every train journey from now on?'

'Mmmm, maybe...'

Aimee was really quite easy to please.

As we headed back across the gardens, towards our families, the skies churned and deepened in colour, but I was euphoric.

I turned excitedly to Helene and the others but they were gone.

'Helene? Aimee?'

Silence.

My fingers went up instinctively to my lips. There was a strangely metallic taste in my mouth and a scratching like knives at the back of my throat. I tried to call out but the only sound that came was a chronic, shredded rasp.

The skies began to rumble as clouds slowly twisted into a maelstrom of whirling fog. Oily, acrid fumes swept over me. I tried to scream, but there was nothing and no one, only a long, penetrating screech before the ground beneath me shuddered and split wide open.

I lost my footing and tumbled, deeper and deeper into a chasm of burning, writhing smoke.

'Jaimie … JAIMIE …'

CHAPTER 5

Fleur Blaise

Paris 2009

'How many times did these dreams occur?'

'I lost count. Each time I would wake in a cold sweat and sobbing out loud. I became terrified to sleep. I would feel physically sick. Yet, slowly, the story advanced a little from the previous years, and I had to know more.'

I looked down onto my hands, turning them over and over. 'You see, I had fallen in love ... with Jaimie, just as the girl in my dreams had. I was willing to risk anything ... to see him again.'

'You fell in love with a figment of your imagination.'

'No, it's so much more.'

The therapist sighed, not unkindly. 'Do you want to go on?'

'I don't know. I don't know if you'll believe me.'

'I'm here to listen. I'll try if you try?'

'She haunts me.'

'Who haunts you?'

'She does.'

The therapist sighed,

'Go on.'

One night, I couldn't sleep. Despite it being the height of summer, blasts of icy air crept over me. I pulled my blanket up higher when all at once my body began to quiver and then, more terrifying, my ears filled with shrill, incoherent screaming. I tried to move but my arms became dead weights. I tried to cry out but my jaws were locked shut. I could only lie in my bed, motionless, trapped.

Gradually, the screeching subdued into a strange whispering. 'Oh no, oh no, oh no …' the voice repeated, over and over. The whispers multiplied as they ricocheted around the room from one wall to the other. I wanted to put my hands over my ears. I wanted to scream out for it all to go away. But I was paralysed.

'Then I saw her.'

The therapist leaned forward.

'Who?'

'Her. But it was … me … dressed as her …'

He frowned. 'What was she wearing?'

'A long, sky blue gown. Her hair was swept up. Some trailed around her face. She seemed from another time …'

'The time of your dreams?'

'Yes …'

'Did this apparition … communicate?'

'It ... *she* looked at me for a long time. I couldn't move. I couldn't speak. My body felt like lead.'

The therapist made notes.

'She turned and just seemed to fade away. Then I heard it. A voice. 'Goodnight, petit cheri.' I was terrified. I suddenly realised it was she who had been whispering 'goodnight' to me all these years, when I'd always thought it was my mother.'

'Do you think she wanted something from you?'

'I didn't know what to think. She seemed sad. Heartbroken, even. But I knew she was the young girl in my dreams and my dreams moved forward.'

'How so?'

'The setting changed from summer to winter. The girl was now seventeen years old, with the prospect of marriage …'

'How did you feel about this change?'

'Things were becoming more complicated …'

The therapist closed his notebook. 'You've been through a lot today. Time up, sadly. We'll continue in your next session.'

I left the clinic, a little vexed that my mental health relied on the mechanisms of the clock. Even so, I had to step out into the real world.

If only I knew what was real.

CHAPTER 6

Fleur Blaise

Paris 2009

My salon appointment was for 2:00 pm but I arrived early and seated myself quietly in the waiting area. I momentarily caught my reflection in one of the mirrors and quickly removed the pins which attempted to hold my hair in place. I let it fall loose. I enjoyed the freedoms of late. I feasted on the sights and sounds around me.

The stylists wore black tunics and had their hair coloured, waxed and twisted into all manner of impossible, striking slants. They worked intently, adjusting clips, pinning hair to one side then the other as they angled and sliced. I instinctively reached to release more pins. I was now, with a little help from madame peroxide, the iciest of blondes, complementing the look with the most translucent foundation I could find. I wore wispy kohl mascara to frame my sky blue eyes and shone my lips with pale pink gloss. I smiled inwardly, it was such a summery look to wear in the middle of winter, but it was my look.

The trainee took me to have my hair washed. I closed my eyes and allowed the hot water to cascade over my head and down to the basin where it splashed and swirled. The trainee was chatting but I hardly heard her, instead I enjoyed the lulling sensation of the water and closed my eyes. The splashing become slow and rhythmical, and I imagined I was drifting away on a boat under the moonlight in the middle of nowhere.

CHAPTER 7

Fleur Babineaux

Normandy 1892

'Let's row,' said Jamie. 'I'll take starboard, you take port.'

It was nearly midnight. This year, we had visited my aunt for Christmas and had, as family once again visited the island abbey. We'd slipped out from our lodgings and made our way to the jetty where boats were left tethered overnight. It was nearly a full moon, enough light to see by. The air was crisp with barely a breeze as we slipped away quietly through the lapping waters towards the island. It seemed as though no one else in the world was awake but us and we revelled in the excitement of it all. We reached our destination and tied up the boat. We carried a flask, a roll-up blanket and the boat's lantern. We walked, hand in hand over the sands towards the glazed gardens of the great Abbey. Tiny, drifting flakes of snow appeared.

'Are you ready?' Jaimie asked at the base of the tower stairwell. He raised the lantern and immediately our elongated shadows spread over the walls around us. The only sounds came from erratic screeches of bats and the long, wavering who-o-o's of distant owls. I was shivering with cold and excitement. Jaimie wrapped the blanket around my shoulders. He took my hand and we carefully negotiated each step upwards. It seemed to take us longer than when we had all raced each other to the top four years ago. We didn't speak much as our voices echoed around the stairwell in such an eerie manner it was unnerving. We finally reached the top and were immediately in awe at the brilliance of the moon and the quickening stars against the indigo sky. We felt suspended in the universe, with countless comets and galaxies spinning past us.

Jaimie turned towards me, his eyes shining.

'Well, sweet Fleur Babineaux, the stars are out tonight. Shall we make good on our bargain?'

'I thought we were just … enjoying the view … ' I said, with a mock shrug.

'Salut!' he said. 'So this is what déjà vu sounds like?' His hands slipped around my waist. His expression became serious. 'Fleur, it's always been you, since the first summer we spent together.'

'Is that so, Jaimie Luc Bonner? So now are you going to tell me why you brought a délicat young lady out on a freezing winter's night?'

'Because you're an adventurer, like me. And we are running out of time for adventures.'

He was right of course. He was already a second-year law student at Caen. I had ambitions of my own. Things would never be quite the same again.

'I brought you here because this is where we shared our first kiss,' he said.

I smiled at the memory, feeling the same rush of joy as our first time.

He raised his hand to my face once more to brush away a stray wisp of hair. Then, he linked his fingers through mine and pressed those soft lips to the palm of my hand. He stood back and produced an exquisitely engraved box from his pocket. We looked at each other for a few seconds and he indicated I open it. I carefully worked the clasp and gasped at the contents - a magnificent diamond and sapphire ring.

'Jaimie ...'

The lantern magnified the cut and brilliance of the stones. They glittered in swirling-blue symmetry on the ceiling above.

'I promised I would only open this box once,' he said. 'It belonged to my great-grandmother.'

'But ...'

'I'm going to ask your father, formally, of course, for your hand.'

I measured out my words. 'Jaimie, I have to complete my studies ...'

There was the slightest of pause. The snow flurries outside thickened.

'We both know no institution will take you.' he said. 'I don't know why you insist ...'

'Newnham Hall will take me. Newnham Hall in England takes girls like me. Things are changing, Jaimie. Women are qualifying as doctors and dentists. A woman in America even ran for president ... for president! Why can't a woman with a head for figures go into commerce?'

'It is not the way in France,' Jaimie countered. 'Here, our women are cultured, beautiful ... feminine. You don't seriously want to travel to stuffy old England?'

'You think I wouldn't be cultured, beautiful or feminine if I went to college?'

Jaimie grimaced. 'You are all those things already. I want you to be my wife. I want you to be happy as my wife. I want us to have a family, a future together.'

'We will. After my studies.'

'Then we are promised to each other.'

'Always.'

He sighed. 'I can almost sympathise with those who put Madame Esquiron in that establishment …'

'Oh, I see that you read …

'And you, Fleur Babineaux, read far too much.'

'I know. And it's good that I do. I love you Jaimie. I only ever want to be with you. If you love me, you'll be patient …'

'I do … I will …'

He kissed my forehead and played with my hairpins until they loosened. My hair cascaded down my back. His mouth brushed urgently at the nape of my neck and up to my lips. 'But we cannot wait forever, Fleur.'

I shivered as we clung to each other, barely wanting to break apart.

'Let's stay …' he whispered, 'just a little longer …'

Some time later, we rowed back to land and made our way to our parents' lodgings, without ever being missed.

CHAPTER 8

Fleur Blaise

Paris 2009

'So, the therapist began. 'You were telling me that things were becoming more complicated.'

I sighed. How to explain the inexplicable?

'There are coincidences, too many. In my dreams, Fleur Babineaux's family return to the coast for their summer break. In real life, my family always return to the coast for their summer break.'

The therapist frowned. 'As do many, who've moved to the city from the coast.'

Here goes, I let it all tumble out.

'I have an Aunt Emma. I have cousins. I fell in love with the boy who lives next door to them. His name is Jaimie. He and I are engaged to be married.'

'I see ...'

'He's newly qualified and works in the city as a junior avocat. I've started my studies in commerce.'

'These are coincidences indeed.'

'I knew you would doubt me.'

'It is not my place to have opinions without due assessment of the facts,' he replied. He sat upright in his chair, tapping his notebook with his pen.

'Let's establish what we know. Your room is inhabited by the apparition of a young woman who has bid you goodnight since childhood. We can surmise she is the Fleur that also inhabits your dreams ... and that she existed around the 1890s. You have a similar set up in terms of family and logistics. She is in love with Jaimie Luc Bonner, whom you appear also to be smitten with. And your Jaimie? Is your Jaimie aware of your double life?'

'She inhabits my nightmares,' I replied, ignoring his question. 'My nightmares.'

The therapist looked at me intently. 'It appears then, that your life and hers are very much paralleled.'

'How can that be?' I sighed.

'Have you thought of the possibility that your real-life anxieties are manifesting themselves through your dreams?' he asked.

'Not every incident in my dreams ... my nightmares, exactly parallels my life. But there are so many ... *too* many coincidences ... with so much detail of another time I couldn't possibly know.

And the apparition in my room ... why would I be visited all these years by a lingering phantom from the past?'

'Phantoms? Spirits? Not at all my field of expertise. I'm here to help you deal with your anxiety, based upon the facts as you present them. I can't help you when it comes to beings from another realm.'

He was right, I needed someone with specialist knowledge.

CHAPTER 9

Fleur Babineaux

Paris 1892 -1895

Despite misgivings on both sides, Jaimie did ask my father for my hand in marriage. My parents would rather me marry sooner than later, but I would have none of it. My fiancé was prepared to wait and that was all that mattered. I pursued my studies in a time when it was neither proper nor fashionable for young women to have careers other than needlework or raising children. Jaimie qualified and commenced at a Parisienne law firm, with excellent prospects. We decided we would marry later that year, following summer break and completion of my own studies.

That September was to be one of the happiest times of my life. I could still hear the squeals of delight from my mother and sisters on the day of the final fittings at the Lafayette. Mme Véronique and her assistants fussed and tugged at waistbands, sleeves and hems to make sure absolutely nothing was amiss. Happy with the bridesmaids, it was my turn. I was whisked away to a private dressing room, and, in front of a floor to ceiling mirror, surveyed my own reflection. In my gown of ivory lace and gossamer, I should only feel beautiful but instead my nerves churned. Was the waistband right? Were the sleeves too long? Should I have chosen the silk brocade?

I could look no more. Mme Véronique sensed my mood and smiled with calm efficiency as she applied herself to my gown and then my hair. Finally, I stepped out, in my veil, for the first time, a bride to be. My mother was rapturous. The bridesmaids were delirious. The assistants cooed.

'Fleur, Fleur, you look like a fairy princess!' cried Lottie, my youngest sister, six and a half years old.

'You look lovely too, little Lottie Locket!' I said, sweeping her up in my arms. She shrieked with laughter as we spun round and round.

The time approached and in October, weeks before the wedding, Jaimie had to leave Paris, suddenly, on business.

'It's only Rouen, a few hours away. I'll be back sooner than you can blink,' he said as we waited on the station platform.

He smiled as he brushed away trailing wisps of hair from my face. 'Those hairpins of yours never work.' We wrapped our arms around one another and said our goodbyes. I remained on the platform, watching as the train curved, under a surge of steam, all the way out of sight.

We received the news from Adrien, the brother of my fiancé, only five days before the wedding. He and his mother had been notified by a representative from the railways, and an officer from the Sûreté accompanied him now.

'I am so sorry to bring you this unbearable news. Our only comfort is that Jaimie could not have suffered. It was all over in minutes.'

CHAPTER 10

Fleur Blaise

Paris 2009

I'd just managed to get to the platform when my phone rang. It was Jaimie.

'Where've you been, we were going to send a search party!'

Spending,' I laughed. 'Spending.'

'Spending? You're supposed to be a penniless student!'

'Yes, but Papa let me have a little extra money!'

'You *could* shop online rather than traipse around in this weather…'

'THAT would be no fun at all …'

'So, besides missing my calls, have you got me anything nice?'

'You'll have to wait and …' His train was arriving. It scraped and screeched across the lines. 'Oh my God …'

'Are you alright? Speak to me, Fleur … what's that noise?'

'It's okay, it's nothing, just your train coming in.'

'You're at the station? No, Fleur, I've been trying to reach you, I'm not on that train. I have to stay in Rouen another day or two.'

'Oh no, why?'

'Theo's been unwell. Vital meetings. I have to fill in for him.'

CHAPTER 11

Fleur Blaise

Paris 2009

'Do not apologise, cheri, so many want to reach out to their dearly departed ... I would surely be out of business if it was not the case!'

'Even so, I appreciate you seeing me at such short notice, Madame Richet. I don't know where else to turn.'

'But of course! Sit down, cheri. Some camomile?'

'That would be wonderful.'

Madame poured.

'Let's get to know one another, cheri. Shall I go first?'

I raised my cup to my lips. Madame smiled. She needed no more incentive.

'At the age of five,' she began, 'each night, after my mother said goodnight and left the room, my bedside was surrounded by what I thought were friendly relatives. I couldn't understand how they just seemed to appear! I was not afraid of them. I just accepted it. But I knew something wasn't right.'

'That's so strange …'

'It was cheri, it was. Some were standing. Some were sitting. The women drank tea from china cups and the men smoked cigars! It was as though they were holding court, each talking, each smiling, each appearing to be so proud of me. But their clothes and mannerisms were not like anything I'd ever seen.'

'You weren't frightened?'

'I saw them less and less as I grew older, but I still heard stray voices and whispers. I coped by telling myself it was only ever my over-active imagination. Then, after my mother died, I came across fading family photographs from a trunk in the attic. I'd never seen them before. Yet I recognised each and every one of the faces of my great-aunts and uncles who came to sit by my bedside all those years ago.'

I was grateful to keep sipping the camomile.

'How incredible ... '

'It was, and quite disturbing, yet I knew they meant me no harm. So, I had no fear of spirits or the unknown. Time went on. The voices returned, not just those of my family, but many, many others ... complete strangers ... There could only be one explanation,' she paused, as if for dramatic effect. 'I had the gift.'

'The *gift*? So what did you do?' I asked.

'What if you could speak to your dear departed and they to you? A few last words, some answers, an au revoir? I could help people. It was to be my vocation. So I set up my parlour, as you see here.'

I thought for a few seconds about the medium's story.

'Do you think ghosts really do linger?'

She shrugged. 'Veiled and beautiful melancholic spirits wafting through the physical world? It has become cliché. Yet they are with us. They communicate every day. Some are happy Some sad. But, we cannot escape them.'

'My visitor ... she isn't ... wasn't a relative, at least I don't think so. But she *is* lingering ...'

'They will often attach themselves to what was once their home. They can be confused, in shock, despairing, depending on the manner of their demise. I fear she may have been waiting a very long time to find the right ... vessel to help her.

'To help her?'

'To cross over, cheri, to cross over.'

'I don't see what I can do, Madame. It's making me ill. I don't understand any of it.'

'Have another sip of your camomile, cheri, and tell me everything.'

I described events from the beginning as much as I could, right up to my final dream, the visit from Adrien and the officer from the Sûreté.

Mme Richet was turning it all over very carefully in her head. Then she spoke. 'This is disturbing. Indeed, she waits till you sleep. She even whispers goodnight before she infuses your dreams with her memories.'

'Sometimes, I don't know if I'm dreaming or not. I walk the streets and I don't know if I'm seeing things with her eyes or mine ...'

'Extraordinary. She possesses your consciousness while you sleep ... and while you are awake.'

'Possesses me? I'm possessed? What does she want?'

'We shall ask her just that,' said Mme Richet. 'I don't think she means you harm. Or it would have happened by now. Yet she wants something only you can give her. Enough. We will summon her. We will find out once and for all what your Fleur Babineaux wants.'

I thanked Mme Richet and left. I would be back. I didn't know if I felt worse or better.

But now, I had something to occupy me, until Jaimie's return.

CHAPTER 12

Fleur Babineaux

Paris. 1895, 2015 & 1895

The awful, awful words of that day never quite left me:

'I am so sorry to bring you this unbearable news. Our only comfort is that Jaimie could not have suffered. It was all over in minutes.'

The shock was so great I maintained mourning for over twelve months, becoming a virtual recluse. It was being with my sisters and particularly, Lottie, which coaxed me back out again, a café here, a restaurant there, a park, a zoo, shopping excursions and even the theatre. I followed them wherever they went. **Over time**, I learned to put my grief behind me.

The summer held mixed memories for me and I could not bear the autumn. I only looked forward to the festivities leading up to Christmas. Shopping on the Rue Tronchet was still, so many years later, compulsory. Here, as always, I would hover over the counters of each elegant boutique or salon and find everything I needed to surprise and delight my mother and younger sisters. I spent hours, handpicking perfumes, scarves, soaps and all manner of trinkets.

The sky dimmed. My eye caught the brightly lit café near the Madeleine. I ordered a warming vin chard, took a table outside and immersed myself in the spectacle of twinkling lights and passersby, all caught up in the throes of their last minute shopping.

I sat here, mesmerised by the beauty of the silent, falling snowflakes and thinking only of the future. The crisp chill in the air and the plethora of Christmas illuminations made me feel truly alive. I was not going to succumb to the nightmare of my past life. Nothing would spoil this night.

I decided I would head towards the fountains of the Place de la Concorde. I spun around each fountain several times to take in the shimmering sea gods, tritons and nereids in all their splendour. I felt delicious, chilling shudders as the snowfall thickened. What next? Should I go for the hustle and bustle of the Champs-Élysées or follow the crowds who strolled through the Tuileries to see the carousel.

I chose the latter.

The trees, lamps and pathways were nearly obliterated by coverlets of fresh snow. Excited children called out in delight as the icy waters of Grand Bassin Rond promised to set. The sound of the jaunty organ churning out Christmas carols drew everyone to the swirling, bright lights of the carousel. I found a bench and sat down to watch the happy faces of the children as they clamoured to ride the painted horses. I couldn't take my eyes off them as they went round, and round and round. I started at the long screeching noise and the sound of crashing steel and concrete and the obliterating smoke. Yet nothing had changed in front of me. The little ones were still laughing and chattering. Would the nightmares I shared with Fleur Blaise never leave me?

I don't know how long I remained. The gardens were deserted. The carousel was silent. The lamplight was barely visible and the moon played hide and seek through dark, churning clouds.

I should leave. I rose from my bench to head towards the fountains but the heel on my boot crumbled. I lost my balance and my bags hit the ground, with me closely following.

He appeared out of nowhere. A tall, gallant stranger who helped me to my feet and gathered up my shopping.

'Thank you, Monsieur, so much. How kind of you,' I babbled.

He seemed surprised. 'It's my pleasure. You're out late? It's nearly midnight.'

Now I was surprised.

'I'm afraid I've been carried away by the shopping, the lights, the ambience ...'

He looked at me long and hard. 'Even so, you shouldn't be out here on your own.'

'I'm not sure where I'm supposed to be right now. I should probably be going ...'

'I'm sorry ... ' said my new companion.

'No, I'm sorry, I'm taking up too much of your time.'

'Allow me, my name Luc ...'

'You must pardon me, Luc. I'm not used to engaging in conversation like this ... not for a while, anyway.'

He looked at me for a few, drawn out seconds, and then sighed. 'I came to the gardens tonight … to find a little peace amongst the madness of this time of year.'

I marvelled that we could see each other and hear each other. A ghost only goes through the motions when feigning what she did in life. No one really sees her or hears her. Not unless she wants them to.

He continued to look at me, quite intently. I thought he was going to say more but he seemed to think better of it.

'We should call a cab,' he said.

'Really, there's no need. I'll go back to the fountains and … '

'No, I insist.'

His gaze was disarming and he spoke so kindly I could not refuse. The snow continued to fall and he held an umbrella over us. I found myself linking my arm through his. He didn't seem to mind. We made our way slowly back towards the Place de Concorde. We spun around the fountains and to the edge of the pavement, on the lookout for a passing cab. My vision became clouded. I clutched tightly onto Luc's arm. Oh no. Please not now. Again, the deafening sound of steel colliding into masonry. The awful, crushing sensation. A woman screaming. Men bellowing instructions. I buried my head into Luc's shoulder.

'You're tired. The traffic's ridiculous. But we won't give up,' my companion said, brushing a wisp of my hair back with his fingertip.

I began to feel a little better at the side of my gallant gentleman. I felt he had questions and so did I.

Before we could speak further, he managed to hail cab and I had to step inside. I turned to thank him, but he was gone.

I think I'd expected it.

I leaned back in the cab and closed my eyes.

Memories from another century flooded through.

Jaimie had travelled to the port of Rouen and would be arriving back, on the Granville to Paris Express, late in the afternoon. I would meet him at the station, and from there we would go to dinner. I arrived early to browse through the emporiums on the upper tier before heading towards the platforms.

I returned home. Alone. My mother and sisters were busy going about their early evening as usual and it wasn't until Adrien arrived at our front door, with the officer from Sûreté, that I realised anything was wrong.

'I'm sorry to bring you this unbearable news. Our only comfort is that they could not have suffered. It was all over in minutes.'

The words played over and over in my head with renewed intensity.

'Our only comfort is that *they* could not have suffered …'

I thought I would burst.

'Jaimie ... JAIMIE!'

It all came back to me with terrifying clarity.

My fiancé had been killed, trapped inside screeching, tumbling carriages.

On making my way to the platform, I too, lost my life, caught under the steel and iron of the runaway train.

My lover was gone. His spirit passed.

But for me, Fleur Babineaux, I was trapped in the ether, invisible to all those around me. My soul had left this body, but not this world.

What sound does a ghost make when it screams?

CHAPTER 13

Fleur Blaise

Paris 2009

'Cheri, you are here. Everything is ready. Come through. Is your phone switched off?'

We went through to a small, ornately decorated parlour. There was an oval table adorned with a purple and gold velvet fringed table cloth. There were two seats. In the middle of the table was a silver candelabra with crystal pendants. Madame Richet lit the candles. We sat down, facing one another, hands linked across the table.

'We'll close our eyes and I will count backwards from ten. Then there will be absolute silence. I need to concentrate on your aura, and through that find hers. Whatever happens your eyes must stay closed.'

'We're not going to … summon her?' I asked.

'No, if she shares your consciousness, she will be here already. She knows we mean her no harm. Our purpose is for her to trust me.'

'I don't know if she *is* here …'

'We will find out.'

We counted backwards. Then silence.

I tried to clear my head but my thoughts raced. Would Fleur Babineaux really appear in this parlour with a stranger? What would we do if she did?

Madame Richet's breathing became slow and steady. I tried to follow suit. I desperately wanted to open my eyes but I dare not risk anything that might chase the spirit away. I wanted answers. I wanted freedom.

We must have sat in silence for ten minutes or more. Madame's breathing was barely audible. I allowed my mind to drift back through my various dreams. The train journeys. Maman, Papa, Aimee, Elise, Lottie. Granville. The harbour. Aunt Emma, Helene. Jaimie. The picnics. The island Abbey. The tower. The kiss. The darkening skies. Crunching masonry. Smoke. Screams.

'No ...' Madame Richet cried out.

'Madame!' I gasped, still not opening my eyes.

'No … You will not … not this way … ahhh …'

I had to open my eyes.

She was covered in sweat. 'We must stop,' she gasped. 'It is over.'

'What do you mean, what happened?'

'She has told me everything.'

'How? I heard nothing …'

'Her consciousness was not with you this day for a reason. She was with me. I understand everything. Now she is gone.'

'Gone? How do you know?'

'She knew what I was trying to do.'

'Which is?'

'Release her spirit.'

'From … ?' I asked.

'I've never come across anything like it before. She's trapped. As though in a vortex. Every time she writhes and turns, she sinks further.'

'Is there nothing we can do?'

'It is a terrible anomaly. She cannot escape. Yet she knows she must leave you. You are both only reliving the nightmare, over and over.'

'And that's it?'

'There's more. Jaimie Luc Bonner was on the express train from Rouen to Paris when the brakes failed and it hurtled through the upper concourse. It plunged through the masonry, down to the pavement below. Fleur Babineaux had gone to meet him. He was *killed* instantly … and so was she.'

'Oh, God, no …' The nightmares were making sense, in the most terrible way. I couldn't help feeling heartbroken. Jaimie Luc was long gone … Then I thought of my Jaimie. Madame must have read my mind.

'You need not worry, history will not repeat itself.'

'How can you know?'

'She never wanted you or your loved ones harmed.'

Nonetheless, I turned on my phone. To my relief there was a message from Jamie: *Still stuck here. One more day. Call you later XXX*

'Come,' said Mme Richet. It is over for you.'

'But not for her?'

'She is caught between worlds. Tragique. It is out of my scope, I cannot help her. But her spirit will not trouble you again. Put it all behind you. Live your life. Pass your exams. Marry your Jaimie. You have everything to look forward to.'

As happy as I felt, I knew I would always think of the handsome young Jaimie Luc, but even more so, of poor Fleur Babineaux.

CHAPTER 14

Fleur Babineaux

Paris 1895 and 2015

Over a century passed since the Montparnasse derailment of 1895. The brakes failed and the train careened through the concourse and plummeted, over thirty feet, down to the pavement below.

My spirit rushed back to my mother's house, and, as though in a dream, I watched events unfold. I saw my family mourn over me and listened as my younger sisters cried themselves to sleep.

I was heartbroken. I began to fool myself that I could mirror an existence alongside my family. Being in the shadows, unseen, unheard, could only be bearable as long as I could see and hear the people I loved. Many years passed. Maman, Papa and my sisters lived out their lives and their spirits passed. I was alone.

With everything lost, most of my time was spent in dormancy. I emerged each Christmas, a spectre, going through the motions, using carefully selected memories to sustain me.

People moved in and out of our apartment until a family from the coast arrived with their young daughter, also named Fleur.

From the first night, I knew I had an affinity with this child. She had relatives on the coast, as I once had. She would travel back each summer, as I once did. I could reach out to her. I could infuse her dreams with my family and the sisters she didn't have in life, and I knew she would want to return to those dreams.

I summoned everything I had to make contact with her one night as she lay in bed, but it went horribly wrong.

I had to implant my consciousness into her dreams.

As she grew older, she met and fell in love with someone called Jaimie. I knew then that my presence was affecting her far more than I could have imagined. My past had merged with her present.

I wanted her to see me, to speak to me and most importantly, through her dreams, relive my fate.

What if the ultimate shared jolt could release her, and my spirit from this world?

She lived my life in the dreams. Over and over. But the jolt of reliving my death proved not enough to release either of us. She had fallen in love with Jaimie Luc Bonner. She wanted the dreams to continue. She wanted to revisit him again and again. She was prepared to go through my death scene over and over just to be with him. I could do nothing. Time went on and took its toll. She was becoming increasing anxious and confused. So was I.

She began slipping out of her time and into mine, losing herself as our lives merged. She was me. I was her. I tried to control it. I would look in the mirror and see her face, her modern day make-up, her hair, falling loose and would vainly try to pin it back up again. My thoughts invaded hers. Hers invaded mine.

My memories with Jaimie were now hers.

I watched them, her and her therapist. She retold and relived my memories but we still remained trapped in the récurrents, no matter their vividness or power.

She sought the advice of the medium, Madame Richet. I realised I could reach out and it was through her that I saw the full effect of my actions.

I had to leave the house that was once home to me and my sisters.

I had to leave Fleur Blaise.

When she returned to Madame Richet, I was there too.

EPILOGUE

Fleur Babineaux

Paris 2015

So, here I am. A spirit, out of place, out of time. My only comfort is to wander through the falling snows of Christmas each year.

I think about Jaimie constantly, I wear his ring, but I must accept that his spirit passed, while mine did not.

Now, at last, I'm more than a pale entity, trapped between worlds. This Christmas, a stranger appeared from nowhere. He walked alongside me. He saw me. He heard my voice.

He wanted to tell me something. Was he trapped too? I longed to find out.

I'll come back, next Christmas and every Christmas. I'll shop and go to the café. I'll pass the fountains on the way to the Tuileries. I'll hover in the shadows and my heel will crumble again. He'll appear and offer to help again, and I'll tell him who I am again. And what I am.

If, like me, he is a spirit trapped, then here, in the late night sanctuary of these exquisite gardens, we have each other.

* * * * *

THE END

Fleur is taken from an upcoming collection of short stories exploring rituals, whether a euphoric gathering on the summer solstice or strange events on a winter's night.

ALSO AVAILABLE BY SUSI MOORE

LEVANA'S WISH

THE SECRET BALLROOM

COMING UP

LEVANA'S DREAM

CREATE & WRITE!
INSPIRATION
FOR
ASPIRING AUTHORS

REVIEW EXTRACTS

http://amzn.to/2b7NbAu
(AMAZON UK)

'IMMERSIVE READING FROM START TO FINISH ...'

'I REALY ENJOYED THIS GHOSTLY TALE ...'

'MS MOORE HAS A DELICATE, ALMOST ETHEREAL EYE ...'

'I LOOK FORWARD TO THE REST OF HER COLLECTION.'

'KEPT ME GUESSING UNTIL THE END ...'

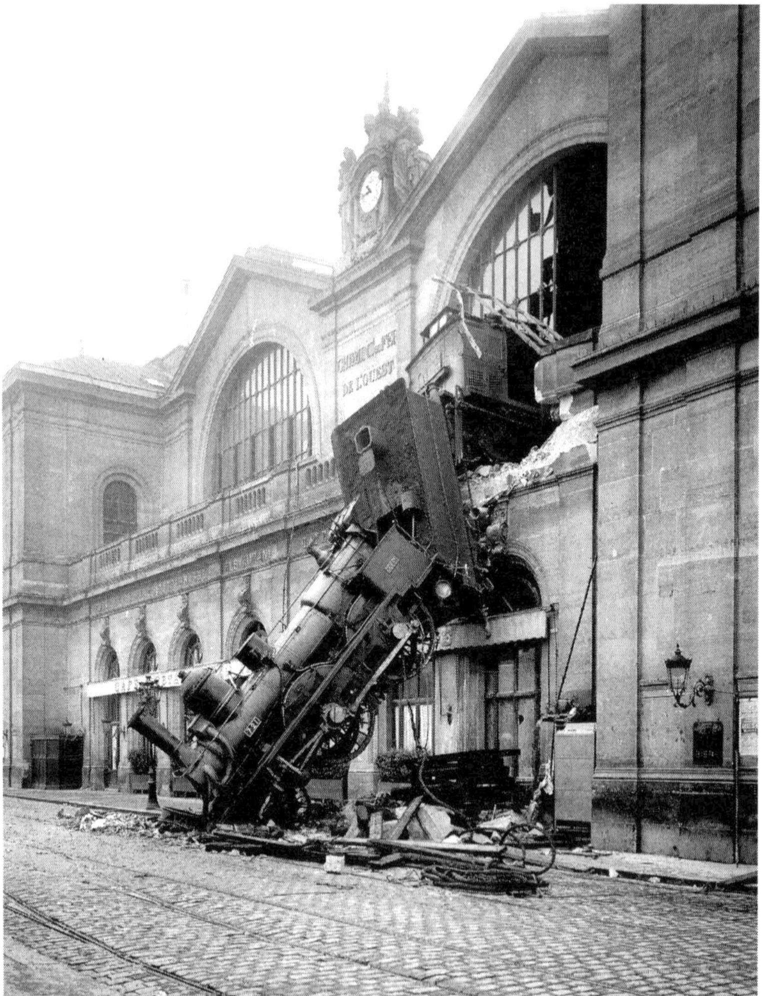

IMAGE: ND/ROGER VIOLLET/GETTY IMAGES

NOTE: *This is a work of fiction and as such, I have taken liberties. The Montparnasse derailment occurred at 4:00 pm on 22nd October 1895, when the air brakes failed. An express locomotive and carriages crashed through the station wall before tumbling 33 feet down onto the Place de Rennes below. Remarkably, there was only one fatality, a young woman, crushed by falling masonry.*

For startling photographs of the runaway locomotive, follow this link:

http://on.mash.to/2aU29Zs

SOME MILESTONES FOR WOMEN:

1855

Elizabeth Garrett-Anderson - first woman to qualify as a doctor (UK)

1866

Lucy Hobbs Taylor - first women to qualify as a dentist (USA)

1872

Victoria Woodall - first woman to run for President (USA)

1887

Susanna Madora Salter - elected Mayor of Angonia, Kansas (USA)

1898

E Mary Charles qualifies as an architect (UK)

1902

Maggie L Walker - first female Bank President (USA)

2007

Christine Legarde - first female Minister of Finance (France)

Extra reading:

*Women's Access to Higher Education (An Overview)
1860 - 1944 - HerStoria*
http://herstoria.com/?p=535

*Voices from the Asylum (Four French Women Writers
1850 -1920)
- Susannah Wilson*
http://bit.ly/2bduQnG

FOR MY FAMILY
AND THOSE SPECIAL TO ME

Fleur © 2016 Susi Moore. All Rights Reserved.
ISBN 978-1542441025

No part of this work or publication may be reproduced
in any form without the prior written permission
of the copyright holder.

Susi Moore asserts her moral right to be
identified as the author of this work.

MUSE, IMAGINE,
CREATE & WRITE ...
© 2016 Susi Moore

Susi Moore's upcoming collection of stories is for lovers of supernatural, romantic and literary fiction.

Titles include 'Levana's Wish', the double-category award-nominated 'Fleur' and 'The Secret Ballroom'.

Ms Moore has been writing since she can remember. She received early acclaim when her music teacher once asked her to stand on a chair and improvise a story to occupy a (quite) fractious end of year class! More recently, as well as her day job and raising a family, she's produced writing workshops for her local college, designed an online course for E-Novelist, runs 'MuserScribe', (musings for aspiring writers) and tends to the whims of her artful felines, Marley and Tabitha.

She's currently working on several projects, including completion of her anthology.

Susi Moore - Amazon UK:
<http://amzn.to/2b7NbAu>

Susi Moore - Amazon USA:
<https://www.amazon.com/author/musermoore>

Website:
<https://susiwritingmooreuk.wordpress.com>

For author updates, musings, original writing prompts and more:
<https://twitter.com/MuserScribe>

© 2016 Susi Moore

ESPECIALLY FOR
MY PARENTS,
JOHN & VERA
WHO LOVED PARIS

© MUSERSCRIBE PUBLISHING

THE STARS ARE OUT TONIGHT

Printed in Great Britain
by Amazon